NEAR THE EDGE

DIANE BYINGTON

Mother Lode Press

Mother Lode
Press

Published by Mother Lode Press
Boulder, CO
motherlodepressboulder@gmail.com

ISBN: 978-0-578-77231-8

Cover design by: Erica Lucke Dean

Printed in the United States of America

"Sometimes, life will take you to the edge, but love of life will bring you back again."

Anthony T. Hincks

CONTENTS

INTRODUCTION

Most of us know what it's like to be too near the edge of a metaphorical cliff. Maybe it feels dangerous or ultra-exciting. Our hearts beat faster, colors are more intense, and the temptation is strong to take that next step and see what will happen. Maybe we do or maybe we don't, but either way, the edge is a real thing.

For me, being near the edge means I'm no longer in control of myself and I'm close to saying or doing something I'll regret later: hysterical tirades, running away from the situation, drinking to excess, or thoughts of violence come to mind when I'm near my edge. So far, I've avoided doing those things, and I think that's largely due to the transformative power of stories. When I'm near my edge, I retreat into stories, either mine or someone else's, and they ground me. Before long, I'm able to behave rationally and face the world again.

The characters in these stories are near their edges. Too near to turn back, in some cases. Falling over the cliff might bring catastrophe and perpetual regret or it might result in transformation. Unfortunately, we don't always know what will happen when we feel the edge crumbling under our toes.

On the other hand, someone—or circumstances—

might help us take a step back from the edge. Something as simple and unexpected as the kindness of strangers or as mundane as a nice day could be the thing that returns us to our usual state of equanimity. In this instance, life will continue on, with only a memory of what might have occurred if we'd taken that next, fatal step into the unknown.

Unfortunately, in these days of COVID and its associated stressors, many of us are all too familiar with the edge. If you're near it right now, I hope these stories will help you back away to safety or show you a way through the chaos until your cooler head prevails. And then, if you choose to step off the cliff, my hope is that transformation will be the result.

Diane Byington

September, 2020

ARMANDO'S REVENGE

For the past two years, the skies had done nothing but rain. Potatoes rotted under the perpetual drizzle, and the grapes tasted foul. If the Torreira family were to keep the farm, someone would have to earn money elsewhere. Armando and his younger brother, Marco, decided who would leave during an all-night conference shortly after burying their father next to their mother. Armando desperately wanted to be the one to go, but how could he ask Marco to care for his wife and two children while he was away for months, even years? In the end, he volunteered to make the sacrifice and stay home. Marco was free to leave.

"Do you really mean it, brother?" Marco stood and clasped his brother's shoulders, searching for anger or deception in his eyes. As boys, they had daydreamed of being explorers, sailing out to sea on a large ship, and returning home rich—heroes. "You would do this for me?"

Armando nodded, unable to speak. The brothers kissed on both cheeks to seal the pact.

Marco's jubilation turned quickly to despair. "Oh, no," he said, tapping his forehead. "There is a problem. I have asked Claudia to marry me and she agreed. Papa gave permission last week, before he grew so sick. With everything that has happened, I forgot to tell you." The excitement drained from his face. "I believe her family will hold me to my promise. She is already twenty-three and may not find another suitor soon."

The brothers sat heavily onto wooden chairs built by their grandfather. They rested their strong arms on the hickory table that had stood in this kitchen for generations. They stared into the fire and thought.

At last Armando said, "You will have to marry, then, before you leave. Claudia can stay here, in your room, until you return with your fortune. We can feed another woman, especially one who works."

"Thank you, 'Mando. I will be forever in your debt." They embraced again.

* * *

And so it was. Marco and Claudia married, and she moved to the farm. Claudia loved playing with the children and cooking the family's meals while Maria Helena, Armando's wife, made cheese to barter in the market. Marco left after the meager harvest was completed, promising to write when he found a ship that would hire him as crew.

Claudia cried for a week, then settled into her new life. She began to sing as she worked. And every day, in the late afternoon while the children napped, she went for a walk that invariably took her to the high cliffs and a view of the sea.

Armando watched her from the corner of his eyes. He noticed her comely figure and long neck, so different from his dumpy, ill-tempered wife. He began to follow her on her walks, remaining far enough back that she didn't see him. He wasn't sure why he did this, but every day he found himself following as she made her way through the trees and up to the cliffs. There, she sang a sad song. She spread her shawl on the ground and sat, staring out to sea, tears streaming down her face.

Armando watched. Weeks later he dared to approach her while she stood near the cliff's edge.

"You," she cried as she whirled to face him. "I am not surprised to see you here. You watch me as if I am a mouse and you are a cat. What do you want of me? Why do you not leave me alone?" Her eyes flashed fire.

"Claudia," he stammered, tentative as he approached her. "Do you not need a man while Marco is away? I could be so good to you." He reached for her hands, staring into her eyes with what he hoped was loving entreaty.

"Certainly not," she snapped, taking a step backward. She was very near the edge. "I am waiting for Marco. If you bother me again I will leave here and return to my parents' home. You will be humiliated, because I will tell them the truth." She glared at him. "Now go, and do not follow me again."

Armando's shoulders sagged. "All right, we will act like this never happened." He reached to take her hand, but she stepped backward and stumbled over a rock. Off-balance, she groped for his arm, but her hand slipped off his shirt. She disappeared over the edge. He heard a single sharp scream and then silence.

Armando stood, frozen, listening for her cries from the river that ran beneath the cliff. If she had fallen into the water, maybe she yet lived. Edging closer, he peered over the rocks. She was not visible, and he heard only the wind. He could not safely climb down the cliff to rescue her. He would have to go around the long way, down the hill and through the fields. He began to run, but stopped when he spotted her shawl on the ground, some distance from the edge. His mind worked feverishly.

If she lived, would she tell about their confrontation? Would she blame him for her fall? And if she died, how would he explain the fact that he had witnessed her fall? How would he explain his presence on her solitary walk?

No, he would avoid all questions by returning to his work in the fields. The longer she was undiscovered the greater the likelihood that she would either die or fail to remember how she came to tumble over the cliff's edge.

He returned to his work, burning off the farthest field, preparing it for spring planting. He returned home at dusk for the evening meal but found no food prepared. His wife had recently returned from the market. The children were unsupervised but appeared to be suffering only from hunger. Claudia was nowhere to be found.

He met his wife's anxious eyes. Together they searched for Claudia, taking a torch to light their way. Eventually they found her body draped in an unnatural position over a rock beside the swollen river. When they knew she was dead, Maria Helena stared up at the tall cliff.

"How could she have fallen? Everyone knows to stay away from the edge. Even the children don't go near."

"I don't know. But obviously she did fall, and I need to carry her inside. Here, take the torch." He gathered his sister-in-law's body into his arms and carried her gently to the house, where he laid her on the kitchen table. Maria Helena prepared her for burial.

Afterward, the village constable questioned family members concerning their whereabouts on the day of the death. Maria Helena was in the village, the children were taking their naps, and Armando was in the far field. He stoutly denied seeing Claudia after the midday meal and hoped he sounded like an innocent man. The constable eventually stopped questioning him and accepted that the death was a regrettable accident. A letter was sent to Marco, but who knew when he would receive it?

Life went on, eventually returning to near normal. Jerking awake from nightmares that came nearly every night, Armando tossed and turned until dawn, seeing again the fear in Claudia's eyes as she stumbled backward to her death. Was he responsible, or had it truly been an accident? If he had found her earlier, would she still be alive? Was he the good man he had always considered himself to be?

He was tempted to unburden himself to the village priest, but fear stopped him. Even if the priest absolved him of guilt, how would he ever hold his head up in the village again? Better to say nothing.

His house became a silent tomb. No one sang now. Maria Helena worked even harder to manage the children, the house, the cheese. She spoke to Armando only of trivialities and silently refused his advances. Increasingly, the children took their chatter elsewhere. The floods of years past gave way to drought. The household grew ever poorer as the years passed and the rain refused to fall on the little farm.

Twenty years passed before Marco returned home. He seemed years younger than his haunted brother and in good humor. He brought gifts, money, and conversation to the house. On his second night home he asked about Claudia's accident. Maria Helena shrugged, glanced at her husband, and retired to bed.

"I cannot tell you what happened, brother. I was working in the fields and Claudia apparently went for her usual afternoon walk. We found her shawl spread on the ground some distance from the ledge. I will show you where it was, tomorrow, if you want. I believe she may have thrown herself off the cliff in her grief from missing you, but I do not know for sure."

Marco was silent, his hands tented under his chin, staring into the fire that had turned to glowing embers. "She was a comely little thing, wasn't she? I wanted her from the first time I saw her. I would not be surprised that any man would want her." His voice was soft and light. "I have thought upon this for years, while I was away at sea. I wonder if she was meeting some man up there. What do you think, brother?" He turned glittering eyes to his brother.

"Uh, well..." Armando could not hold the gaze. "I do not know, for I was away at the time, but I can tell you that no man came around here sniffing after her that I saw. She sang for you, sad, lonely longs. No, I do not think that someone from the village was involved. Perhaps she meant to throw a flower into the river for you and stumbled and fell." He looked at Marco and shrugged, a faint smile on his face.

Marco stared into the fire and waited long before speaking. "As you know, I have not married again, and will not. Many nights I have lain awake, wishing you and I had changed places. Wishing I had my own wife and children, my own cozy little home. You seem to not value your riches, my brother."

Armando snorted. "Riches I have not. Only a silent wife, children who rarely visit, and backbreaking labor for a subsistence living. You have traveled the world, seen amazing things. How could my poor life compare with that?"

"Ah, 'Mando. I wish I had never gone away. She might still be alive, my lovely Claudia." Sighing, Marco reached to add a log to the fire.

* * *

The next afternoon, the brothers carried materials to the cliff's edge to build a bench in Claudia's memory. They sawed and hammered, and when it was completed, Marco sat on the bench and stared over the hills to the sea. "If I had built this before I left, perhaps she wouldn't have needed to stand so near the edge."

Reaching inside his shirt he pulled out a small piece of cloth and showed it to Armando. "Maria Helena gave me this yesterday. She found it in Claudia's fist when she was preparing her body for burial. Did you not have a shirt like this, brother?"

Armando jerked, startled. His other hand felt for the spot on his arm that her fingers had grasped as she fell. He was sure, almost, that she had not torn his shirt. But could it have happened? No, he thought not. His brother was testing him. Quickly he lowered his hand and rearranged his expression to one of disbelief.

"You accuse me? But I was not there. That is not my shirt, I assure you." He hoped his laughter sounded sincere.

Marco nodded. "In a way, I don't blame you for being tempted. She was a lovely thing. I almost did not believe it of you. But you gave yourself away when you grabbed your arm." His voice was grim.

Flicking the piece of cloth onto the ground, he picked up the hammer and started resolutely toward Armando.

The two men grappled, fell, and rolled on the ground as each tried to kill the other. Unbeknownst to either, they were very near the edge. The hammer dropped to one side. Marco crawled toward it, and Armando stood and kicked him in the stomach. Marco fell, gasping for breath, and rolled over the cliff's edge.

Armando could hear Marco's body crashing off the rocks as it made its way to the river and thence to the sea, the screams echoing in the distance. He gathered his tools and whistled, walking slowly around the long way to find his brother.

I wrote this story during a vacation in Portugal. The Portuguese are understandably proud of their history as a seafaring, adventurous nation. While touring through several magnificent museums dedicated to the seafarers, I couldn't help but wonder what it was like for the ones who stayed home and watched their brothers leave with all the glory. Hence, this story. Armando stepped too close to the edge of the cliff to turn back, with catastrophe as the result.

First published in <u>American Fiction: Volume 14</u>, 2015. Morehead, MN: New Rivers Press.

DARYL THE MAILMAN

D aryl liked to wear his Elvis wig when he delivered the mail to his rural route, and in between mailboxes, he practiced for his gigs. He was trying to perfect the little catch in Elvis's voice, and he belted out the phrase, "Don't be cruel," over and over. The postal job itself was boring, but with the wig he didn't have to be Daryl the Mailman. He could be Daryl the Elvis Impersonator.

At the end of this day he noticed a text from Arturo, his supervisor. "Stop in and see me before you leave." Sighing, he wondered what he had done wrong this time. Back at the post office, Daryl stuffed the wig into his locker, tucked in his shirt, and ran his fingers through his mussed hair. He walked through the mostly-empty building, nodding at Carmen, another mail carrier.

"How's it going?" Carmen asked.

"Fine. I guess." He shrugged and rubbed his forehead, trying to rid himself of the headache that had started pounding when he received Arturo's text. He hadn't slept well recently, and he hated to see the expressions of sympathy on his colleagues' faces.

Arturo looked up when Daryl knocked at his office door. "There you are. Have a seat." Daryl pursed his lips and sat. He hoped he wasn't going to get fired. It wasn't easy to fire a postal service employee, though, so that probably wasn't it. Still, something was seriously amiss.

Arturo was a few years younger than Daryl. Maybe forty. He'd shot up the hierarchy from mail carrier to station supervisor in record time. Outside the office he liked to party, but during working hours he was all business. Now he shook his head. "Mrs. Fernandez was in today. She pushed her walker into my office and waved the letter that you didn't pick up in my face. That's the second time this week. What's up?"

Oh, shit. Mrs. Fernandez lived nearly a quarter mile off of Highway 64 on a dirt road. She received so little mail that he sometimes forgot to drive down the pot-holed road and check her mailbox. He couldn't tell his supervisor that he'd been too busy rehearsing to bother, so he opted to pass the blame. "If she would move her mailbox to the main road like everyone else, I wouldn't forget."

"You know we gave her a waiver. She's too frail to walk all the way to the main road, and she doesn't drive. This was her utility bill, and her power almost got shut off because of you. She had to get a neighbor to drive her in so she could pay it."

Daryl's bravado seeped away. "Oh. I'm sorry. I'll do better."

"If you don't, I'm going to have to put you on report. You need to go by her house tomorrow and apologize. And, for God's sake, check her mailbox when you go."

"No problem. I really am sorry."

"Word is that the old lady is a *bruja*," Arturo said, and laughed. "You don't want to piss her off too much, or you might get turned into a toad."

Daryl thought a minute. He'd only been in Chama for

a year. He might have heard that word before, but he wasn't sure. "*Bruja*?"

"Yeah. Some people say she's a healer, but others think she's a witch. I don't know if it's true, but you need to apologize to her. For a bunch of reasons."

"I already said I'd do it. Don't worry."

Arturo nodded, then closed his office door. "All right," he said, sitting back down. "Our conference is officially over. What's really going on?"

Daryl shook his head. "Nothing really. I'm a little jumpy about this gig I've got this weekend. It's the first one since Dolores left." He didn't mention that the divorce papers had arrived in yesterday's mail. If he didn't sign them right away, she might call to find out why. And then he could try and change her mind. But Dolores was unpredictable. He had to think about it some more.

"I know you enjoy being an Elvis impersonator," Arturo said "but you write good songs. Why don't you get a gig singing your own songs instead of impersonating some dead guy?"

"People like Elvis."

Daryl remembered Dolores's biting words as she stormed out the door: "You drink too much. You have no personality. And you can't even sing Elvis right." He didn't disagree. He might not be able to develop a personality that Dolores would like, but if he could just perfect the little catch in his voice, at least he could do Elvis better.

"I think people would like you, too, if they got to know you."

They sat in silence for a few minutes. Finally, Arturo said, "You want to get a beer or something? We should be able to get in at the High Country."

"Nah. I'm not drinking any more. Dolores doesn't

like me when I'm drunk."

"Oh. Okay." He hesitated. "Have you heard from her lately?"

"No." The divorce papers had been from her lawyer, so he wasn't technically lying. "I'm hoping she'll come back if she hears I've stopped drinking."

For a moment, Arturo stared at him with a mixture of pity and tenderness. Then, in a lighter voice, he asked, "Where you playin' this weekend?"

"In a retirement community in Taos. They're celebrating the fiftieth wedding anniversaries of some of the residents. The old people like Elvis songs."

"Well, good luck with it. Hey, come in tomorrow afternoon and let me know how it goes with Mrs. Fernandez, okay?"

"Sure." Daryl trudged out of the office. His head ached and he really wanted a beer, but if he started drinking, he might not stop. Besides, he needed to rehearse.

***

The next morning, Daryl drove to Mrs. Fernandez's mobile home, tucked up against a tall cliff. There was no mail, either outgoing or incoming. He knocked on her door and, after a long moment, it swung open.

Mrs. Fernandez was gaunt, like she hadn't eaten in a while. The old woman held onto the door and swayed. Daryl wanted to grab her to keep her from falling, but he wasn't sure it would be appropriate. He waited, prepared to catch her if she fell.

After a moment she said, "You're the mailman. The Elvis one."

"Yes, ma'am. I'm sorry I didn't pick up your mail yesterday."

The old woman frowned. "That's all right. I took

care of it." She pointed inside and said, "Come in and sit for a few minutes. I haven't had a visitor recently."

Daryl was too busy to sit and visit, but he couldn't turn the old woman down. "Uh, okay. Just for a minute." He walked into the home, past the avocado green washer and dryer, past the cat dish with dried food stuck on the side, and into the living room, where a game show filled the giant TV screen. The sound was so loud that he nearly covered his ears, but he stopped himself. Even if he didn't have a personality, at least he could be polite.

Mrs. Fernandez clicked off the TV. The quiet was startling. Daryl could hear red-winged blackbirds singing outside, and the sound of a plane that was probably headed to the Albuquerque airport. He sat on the edge of a faded blue recliner, and a grey cat jumped onto his lap. Mrs. Fernandez lowered herself onto a patched green sofa.

Looking around the room, Daryl noticed half a dozen African-type wooden masks hanging on the walls. He'd seen masks like these on "Antiques Roadshow," and, if he remembered correctly, they'd been worth a lot. A paper Lone Ranger-type mask was tacked to the wall behind the couch. *Strange.*

Daryl wanted to ask about the masks, but he forced himself to look at the old woman, who was staring at him with a twinkle in her eyes. He felt his clammy skin heating up as he tried to figure out how to proceed. He'd never been inside one of his customers' homes before. This one wasn't clean, but it was habitable. Maybe as clean as his own home, now that his wife wasn't around to remind him to clean it.

Finally, he cleared his throat. "Like I said, I'm sorry about missing you yesterday, and the other times, too. I'll do a better job of looking for your mail in the future."

Mrs. Fernandez nodded. "You might not believe this, but I was young once. I did a lot of things back then. Waitress. Cook. I liked being out and about." She looked at Daryl expectantly.

Daryl wondered what she wanted of him. With the exception of the masks on the wall, she seemed to be an ordinary old woman, almost like his grandmother back in Atlanta. He wouldn't have taken her for a famous witch. Or rather, *bruja*.

"That's great, ma'am. It's nice to be outside and not stuck behind a desk all the time. I like that, too." He hesitated, then started to rise. "Sorry I can't stay and visit. I've got to deliver other people's mail." The cat tumbled off his lap. He tried to wipe off the cat hairs that had stuck to his blue uniform shorts, but realized that was rude. No matter, he had a rag in the truck. "I can let myself out," he said. "No need for you to get up." He walked to the sofa and reached down to shake her hand. "Nice meeting you, ma'am. Have a good day."

A streak of lighting ran up his arm when their hands touched. "What the..." He immediately jerked his hand away and shook it, trying to get the feeling back.

Mrs. Fernandez pulled herself to a standing position. "What's wrong, son? Can I help you?"

"I... something happened when we shook hands. A shock or something."

The old woman frowned. "I wonder if that was because of my heart defibrillator. It sometimes goes off and shocks me, but I've never known it to shock another person. I'm sorry if I hurt you."

Her explanation didn't make sense. His father had a defibrillator, and it didn't shock anyone. The trailer's floor seemed to roll under Daryl's feet. He needed to get out of there quick. "Uh, no problem. See you later." He moved toward the door.

"Wait a minute, *mijo*," she said. "I've got something for you." She pushed her walker into the kitchen. Reaching into an upper cupboard, she pulled down a plastic bag filled with something that looked like dried weeds, then poured a portion of it into a brown paper bag. She turned to Daryl. "Here. Try this for a few days. It might help you."

"No thank you, ma'am. My arm's getting better already." But it wasn't. It felt numb all the way up to his shoulder.

She nodded like she understood he was lying but didn't want to call him on it. "I didn't mean to hurt you. But this will help."

Trying to look grateful, he took the bag. "Uh, what is it?"

"Tea. After you boil a cup of water, put in one tablespoon of this and let it steep for ten minutes. Then drink it. It'll make you feel better."

"Thank you." He turned to leave.

"And come back in a week and let me know how it worked." She laughed. It wasn't exactly a witchy cackle. But close.

Outside, he breathed a sigh of relief and got into his truck. There was no way he was going to drink that tea or come back to see that old lady. She might or might not be a *bruja*. One thing was certain, though. He would never again forget to pick up her mail.

The numbness in his arm receded as the afternoon wore on. He wished he had someone to tell about the strange encounter. If his wife had been home, he would have told her. Back at the post office, he knocked at Arturo's door. His supervisor waved him inside. "How did it go?"

"Your frail little old lady just tried to kill me. She shocked the shit out of me when we shook hands. My arm still feels strange."

"What?"

When Daryl finished telling the story, Arturo shook his head. "I think maybe she was playing one of her tricks on you. She's kind of famous for them. I'm glad you're okay. Strange things happen back in these hills, my friend. Land of Enchantment and all that. You're not in Georgia anymore."

"I'm okay. Hey, you want to go to the park and watch the sunset?"

* * *

The next Saturday night, after Daryl had sung all his Elvis songs and received a standing ovation for "Don't Be Cruel," he took a deep breath and said, "I wrote this one. Hope you enjoy it."

It was a new song, one he'd written in the past week. Deep love and loss were his realities, and the words reflected his longing for his wife. To his ears, he sounded like a lonesome wolf howling in the desert. Not at all like Elvis.

When he finished, the applause was scattered. A few people cried. Others seemed confused.

This had been a disaster. He should have chosen a more upbeat song. But he didn't have any of those. So he ended with a fast Elvis song, and everyone seemed relieved.

He didn't know why he'd tried out one of his songs on this group. Maybe it was because of the pretty activities director who smiled at him from the corner of the room. He wanted her to think of him as more than a guy in a greasy black wig and a sparkling suit. He looked for her after his last song, but she was nowhere to be seen.

"Figures," he thought. "People would rather have Elvis than Daryl. I knew it all along."

On Sunday evening, his phone rang. Dolores, at last. He tried to keep from sounding too eager when he answered.

"I just called to tell you that I'm getting married again," she said. "Have you signed the papers yet?"

Married? She'd only been gone for five weeks. And they'd been together for eight years. "I don't understand. We're not even divorced yet."

"So what?"

Leaving his computer programming job in Atlanta and moving to New Mexico apparently hadn't been enough to sustain their marriage, then. He tried to think of what to say, then settled on, "Uh, do I know him?"

"No, you don't know him. I'm livin' in Denver now. How many people do you know in Denver?"

"None."

"All right, then."

He paused. "I stopped drinking after you left."

"That's good. But it wasn't just the drinking that made me leave. It plain didn't work between us, Daryl. We're different people, is all. I know you moved to Chama to help me take care of Mama, but she's dead now. I couldn't stay there. You don't have to, either."

"I'll move to Denver if you want me to."

"How many times do I have to tell you?" Her irritation was loud and clear. "It's over with us. You need to move on with your life. I have."

He sighed. "All right. I'll give the papers to my lawyer and see what he says."

Dolores snorted, like she knew he didn't have a lawyer. "You do that."

After they hung up, he stared at the phone for a long while. Then he went out to the garage and tinkered with his motorcycle. Later, he drove to the liquor store and bought a fifth of vodka. Back home, he set the bottle on the counter and stared at it. He wanted to drink the whole thing at one sitting. Drink until he passed out on the floor. If he inhaled his own vomit and died, so be it.

He fingered the one-month chip from AA that he kept in his pocket.

He stared at that bottle for a long, long time. Then he noticed the bag of tea Mrs. Fernandez had given him. He'd dropped it onto the counter when he'd gotten home that day and hadn't thought about it since. A voice in his head said: *Why not try it?*

His arm turned numb just as it had when he had shaken her hand. To distract himself from the vodka, he brewed up the tea and took a sip. It tasted like the chamomile tea his mother had given him when he had an upset stomach as a kid. Strange to taste it now, so many years later. He added honey and drank the entire cup. It warmed his heart as well as his stomach. And it seemed to erase the headache that had been his constant companion for weeks.

When he went to bed, the vodka was still sitting on the counter, unopened, and he felt a little better.

At work the next day, instead of playing Elvis songs in his truck, he played an old recording by Leonard Cohen. His favorite song on the album was "Suzanne." His first girlfriend had been named Suzy, and he wondered what had happened to her.

The day was one of the most beautiful he could remember. Aspen trees quaked in a light breeze and sent their orange and yellow leaves drifting onto his truck.

Snow might arrive later in the evening. Even if things weren't working out at the moment, he was still glad he'd moved to New Mexico.

Mrs. Fernandez's front door was closed, and there was no mail, in or out. He hoped the old lady was all right, but he didn't stop. She'd probably forgotten that she'd asked him to return.

Back at home, he found a check in his mailbox from the retirement home. The activities director had included a note with the check. "Thank you so much for your concert last Saturday. The residents particularly loved that sad song you played near the end. At least half a dozen people have asked me to get you back to sing more songs like that. They like Elvis, but that song really spoke to them. What do you think?"

She'd signed the note, "Suzanne." *Strange.* He hadn't known her name.

He drank another cup of tea. The next day he took the vodka to work and handed the bottle to Arturo, who grinned and thanked him.

Every evening during the next week, Daryl wrote down the songs that came to him as they drifted by. He signed the divorce papers and sent them back. His colleagues started smiling at him without sympathy in their eyes.

The next Saturday night he returned to the retirement home and sang his own songs. Although most of them were sad, he discovered that his own well of sadness wasn't as deep as it had been. People clapped hard after every song, often with tears in their eyes. By the end of the concert, he knew his days as an Elvis impersonator were over.

Suzanne thanked him and walked him to his car. He

gathered up his courage before speaking. "I come to Taos pretty often. Would you like to get a cup of coffee or something the next time I'm in town?"

She smiled. "Yes."

On Monday, he stopped at Mrs. Fernandez's house. When he knocked at her door, the woman who answered appeared younger than before. She didn't use a walker or sway like she was off-balance. But she was the same woman, Daryl thought, just younger. *What the...?*

"Come in, come in. It's nice to see you."

The trailer was tidy. The cat bowl was newly washed, dishes were clean and stacked in the drainer, and the television was off. Daryl gulped. How could the old woman have changed so much in such a short time? He didn't ask, just handed her a letter from someone in New Orleans.

"Thank you," she said. "Sit down, please. Could I get you some tea?"

"Uh, no thanks. I just came to thank you for the tea you gave me before. It sure helped me. I wonder... could I ask what was in it?"

"As I recall, it was chamomile. I grew it myself." She gestured to a small garden outside the trailer.

"Chamomile? Just chamomile? Nothing, uh, special?"

She laughed. This time it sounded like the tinkle of a music box instead of a cackle. "No, nothing special. You've probably heard the rumors about me. Not true. I'm just a former waitress who lives alone since my husband died. I don't want anybody breaking in, so I allow those rumors to persist."

He had no idea what to say to that. They sat for a while in silence. Finally, she asked, "What's that you're holding?"

He bit his lip, wondering whether he was being foolish. Finally, he decided to go for it. Hoping she wouldn't be offended, he said, "Uh, ma'am, it's the Elvis wig I used to wear. I don't have a need for it anymore. I know it's silly, and feel free to say no, but I wondered if you would want it. You know, for your wall. It's not a mask, I know, but it seems to fit with the others."

She looked up at the wall and nodded. "Thank you, son. It will have its own special place." She took the wig from him and patted it.

As he stood to leave, she asked, "*Mijo*, would you like some more tea?"

"No, I don't think so. I appreciate it, though."

* * *

Soon after, he requested a transfer to Taos. The next year, after their marriage, he told Suzanne the story about Mrs. Fernandez. They drove up on his motorcycle to visit her.

When they arrived, the mobile home was deserted, with tall weeds growing around it and clumps of animal scat in the driveway. The mailbox had been torn down. Daryl parked, and he and Suzanne walked up to the front door. It was open, so they went inside. All of the furniture was gone. No washer or dryer, no cat bowl, no couch or chair, no TV. And no masks on the wall.

Daryl went into the kitchen and opened the upper cupboard. Inside was a brown paper bag filled with something that looked like weeds. The words, "Daryl the Mailman," were written on the side. He pulled down the bag and held it up to his nose. Chamomile tea. It smelled fresh.

"How did she know we were coming?" asked Suzanne, a tone of wonder in her voice. "Do you think she moved down the street or something, and saw us drive up?"

He shrugged. "I don't know. Why don't we ask her neighbor?"

They walked the quarter mile to the next house. Daryl knocked, and a middle-aged woman answered the door.

"Hello," she said. "May I help you?"

Daryl cleared his throat. "I was wondering about Mrs. Fernandez, who used to live down the road. Do you know what happened to her?"

The woman nodded. "Oh, yes. She moved to New Orleans to live with her sister. I correspond with her from time to time. She seems to like it there." She glanced at the bag in Daryl's hands. "Ah, it looks like you've been to the trailer. Did she leave that for you?"

"I... I guess so," Daryl said. "But it looks like it was put there recently. I don't know what to think."

The woman was quiet for a moment. "Mrs. Fernandez is a powerful shaman. Her ways of healing people are... unique, I guess I would say. I wouldn't ask too many questions, if I were you. Just accept the gift and use it when you need it." She peered at him. "Have I seen you before? You look familiar."

"I used to be your mailman."

"Ah. Mrs. Fernandez spoke of you often. You were one of her favorites."

"Favorites?"

Suzanne and Daryl looked at each other, not knowing what to say. Finally, the woman asked, "Would you like her forwarding address?"

Daryl nodded then accepted the piece of paper she handed him. "*Buena suerte*," she said, closing the door.

Daryl and Suzanne walked slowly back to the motorcycle. Daryl would keep the tea in case he ever needed it. For now, though, it would remain unopened in the kitchen cupboard.

He and Suzanne planned to take a trip to Atlanta next summer. After they spent some time with his family, he might suggest they take a couple of extra days and drive over to New Orleans. He'd like to see if his friend was displaying his Elvis wig on her wall.

My husband and I lived for seven winters in a mobile home park in Central Florida, and our mail carrier was also an Elvis impersonator. I never saw any of his shows, but people said they were fun. It occurred to me that most mail carriers spend their days alone in a truck. What a wonderful time to practice songs. And so, Daryl was invented—a transplant from the South to New Mexico. Mrs. Fernandez, either as a sweet old lady or a powerful bruja, helps him step away from his edge, and his new life is a testament to that help.

A version of this story was published in <u>166 Palms: A Literary Anthology</u>. 2018. Pg. 73-87.

THE CHRISTMAS JACKET

E very Christmas is magical in its way, but the Christmas I want to tell you about happened in 1967, when I was fifteen. My parents and I had moved from Ohio to a small town in the center of Florida—Valencia—three months before. We were poor, and my dad drank, so Christmas wasn't going to be much at our house. In fact, if I hadn't thrown a fit, we wouldn't have even had a Charlie Brown Christmas tree that year. My dad was a migrant farm worker and my mom cooked and took care of the old couple who lived in the big house on their farm, while we lived in the tiny cottage beside it. For my parents, Christmas was just a day when they didn't have to work. Mom usually spent it watching sappy Christmas movies on television and Dad would play whiny songs on his guitar and drink beer.

This was going to be a different kind of Christmas for me. For one thing, I'd always experienced snow on Christmas. I knew it wouldn't snow that far south, but Christmas day was forecast to be cold. It would have to do. But hanging Christmas lights on palm trees just felt... wrong.

Because money was so tight, Mom didn't bother to ask what I wanted for Christmas, and I didn't offer. I figured

I would get something small, as usual. I hoped for a record album or a book, maybe even a sweater, but that was about all I could expect.

I didn't dare ask for it, but I was dying for a Valencia High athletic jacket. The jacket was maroon and white and was just the right weight to keep me warm without being too heavy, and it had the school's name embroidered on the back. Some of the athletes also had letters sewn on the front. I was on the track team, but I hadn't been running long enough to earn a letter. Even though my parents didn't approve of my running (that's another story), I was an athlete and I wanted to prove it by wearing one of those jackets. The problem was that they cost $25, which was a lot of money in those days and always would be for poor people like us. I knew I wouldn't get one, so there was no use whining about it. "No use whining about it" was a standard phrase in our house, attributed to everything from store-bought clothes to staying in one place long enough to finish out the school year.

I planned to give my parents a pelican I had carved from cypress wood during the slow days at my after-school job. My friend Francie's Uncle Stan owned the store where I worked, and he had taught me how to carve—sort of. It was my first effort, and I hoped my parents would take that into consideration when they unwrapped it.

On Christmas morning, I woke up early and tiptoed into the living room. "Santa" had left a few things beneath the tree. A quick glance at the shape of the boxes told me I had guessed right. Record, book, probably sweater. I'd open the gifts later, and ooh and ahh over them, but first I wanted to go for a run. I dressed in my usual shorts and tee-shirt but realized my mistake as soon as I walked outside. *Brrr.* Too cold for those clothes. Back inside, I pulled on sweat pants, but I didn't have the right weight jacket. My winter coat was too heavy. What to do? Rummaging through my closet, I found a wool sweater that I'd worn when we lived in Ohio. Moths had eaten holes all over it, so it wasn't fit to wear in public, but it might work for running.

Francie, my running partner and friend, lived a half mile away. I was surprised to see her stretching outside her house when I ran by. "Merry Christmas," I said, running up to her, "I thought you wouldn't be able to run today."

"Hi, Faye. Merry Christmas to you, too. Mom told me to be back in half an hour to start cooking, so I've only got a little while." She peered at me. "What is that you're wearing?"

I felt myself blush. Francie's family was rich. She wouldn't be caught dead wearing a holey sweater. "I know. Ugly. But it'll keep me warm. Come on, let's go."

We ran into town and back. When we returned to her house, Francie said, "Come in for a minute. I want to show you something."

"All right."

She led me into her bedroom and stopped before a large bag that appeared to be filled with clothes. "Mom had Kyle and me go through all our clothes and pick out a bunch of stuff to give to a Cambodian refugee family that are new here. They had to leave their country so fast that they couldn't take anything. Can you imagine? Anyway, I wondered if you wanted to go through it and take what you want before we give it to them." She shrugged. "Mom said it would be okay."

I wasn't sure what to say. Francie's parents were so nice that I didn't think about them being rich very often. Francie and I were about the same size, so her castoffs would be better than my best clothes. But was it the right thing to do?

I was about to decline when I noticed, on top of the bag, what looked like a Valencia High jacket. I couldn't help myself. I walked over to it and picked it up. *Yep.* I hadn't even told Francie how much I wanted one of those.

"You getting rid of this?" I asked, trying to sound casual.

"Not me. It's Kyle's. Now that he's in college, he doesn't want stuff that reminds him of high school." She shook her head. "You're welcome to it."

Oh, gosh. I had only met Francie's brother once before, at their house a couple of months earlier. But he was the cutest boy I'd ever seen and I had a huge crush on him. Now I doubly wanted it. It might smell like Kyle, and I could pretend I was his girlfriend when I wore it. And everybody would know I was an athlete. I'd be warm, too. The jacket was perfect.

But how could I possibly accept this gift? My mom constantly harped that we didn't take charity. Sure, we shopped at Goodwill all the time, but that wasn't charity, she said. It was just smart shopping.

But oh, how I wanted that jacket. I said, "Are you sure it's okay to take this? What about the Cambodian family? Won't one of them want it?"

"I don't know. Mom said I could give you first dibs. There's a couple of other jackets in there, too." She hesitated, as though she was thinking about saying something else. Finally, she said, "I think you should take it. Call it a Christmas present from Santa."

We laughed. I'd stopped believing in Santa at least ten years before.

"All right. Thank Kyle for me, okay?" I peeled off the

holey sweater and dropped it on the floor. "Will you throw that away?" When Francie nodded, I slipped on the jacket and twirled in front of her mirror. It was a size too large, but that felt exactly right. The jacket's arms went past my hands, which would be great when it was cold. And it was long enough to cover my tee-shirts. I would be toasty warm without sweating. The deep maroon color even set off the highlights in my red hair. I held it up to my nose and sniffed. It smelled a little like pine needles. Probably not Kyle's smell, then. It must have been recently dry-cleaned.

I hugged Francie then walked home, luxuriating in my good fortune. Even though I didn't believe in him, Santa had definitely visited me that day.

Mom was making breakfast when I got home. She looked at me with that squinty expression I dreaded. "Where'd you get that jacket?"

I was stuck. If I said it was an old one of Kyle's, Mom would tell me I couldn't take charity and make me give it back. If I said Francie had given it to me, she would tell me it was too expensive and make me give it back. As I saw it, I had no choice but to lie. My mind worked feverishly. Finally, I said, "Francie loaned it to me. I didn't realize how cold it was outside."

She nodded. "That's sweet of her." Turning back to the griddle, she said, "Pancakes will be ready in a couple minutes. Wash your hands and set the table, will you?"

I felt bad about lying to my mom, especially on Christmas. But I wanted—needed—that jacket. I hung it up in my closet and ran my hand down the sleeves. The fabric was so soft that I wanted to rub my cheek on it. I would take the jacket to school and leave it there, so Mom would never know that I hadn't returned it.

We ate pancakes and opened our gifts. Just as I'd

thought, I got a Beatles album, a Nancy Drew book that I'd read years before, and a pretty green sweater. I hugged my parents and told them to thank Santa for me. It was a long-standing joke in my family that Santa brought the gifts, so if I didn't like something I was supposed to blame Santa, not them. They meant well, and I was far mellower about everything since I had that jacket.

They unwrapped the bird. Dad said, "It's a pelican, right? Nice." I was so relieved that I nearly cried when he recognized what it was and liked it. Dad was usually either working or drunk, so he rarely paid any attention to me. At least so far, he was neither, so it was a good day.

I washed the dishes then went to my room to listen to my album while my parents read the newspaper. Afterward, we ate lunch and got ready to go to Francie's house. We'd been invited to join their family for dessert.

Kyle barely noticed my existence, because he was hanging out with his girlfriend, Linda, who turned out to be charming. I tried not to show my disappointment. Francie's dad and her Uncle Stan told stories about the war. They had been best buds all their lives and had been army pilots together. They'd gotten shot down and captured by the Germans. The ordeal had made them even closer friends. The whole afternoon was like a Norman Rockwell painting. Except that Dad got drunk, told off-color jokes, and embarrassed everybody. Same old, same old. Mom took him home early, but she allowed me to stay at Francie's for a while. After they left, Francie's mom, Laney, pulled me into the kitchen, just the two of us. She saw that I was about to cry and handed me a tissue.

"Sit down, honey, I want to talk to you." I sat, fearful of what was going to happen. In a gentle voice, she continued. "Faye, I know it's hard having such a difficult dad.

But what he does, whatever he does, is not your fault. And just because he's like he is doesn't mean that you're going to be like him. Not at all. You're your own person, and you can choose how you want to be. You get to decide. Don't forget that, all right?"

I nodded, unable to speak.

She said, "Now please get Francie. We're ready to leave to see the Christmas lights."

Valencia was known for its display of Christmas lights. I hadn't seen them yet and was so excited I had a hard time sitting still as Francie's dad drove us into town and parked. Kyle had gone over to his girlfriend's house, so it was just the four of us. The town square had been transformed into fairyland—thousands of blinking lights adorned all the trees, the bushes, and buildings. I didn't care that most of the trees were palms. They looked beautiful. The town had even trucked in a little snow so kids could throw snowballs at each other. I walked around, transfixed by the magic of the evening.

The cold had settled in, with the temperature hovering around freezing. If you haven't experienced that level of Florida cold, you won't understand. But it seemed colder even than in Ohio. My new jacket was perfect. I zipped it up and felt warm and toasty.

We walked around the square, marveling at the lights. Three quarters of the way around, Francie's dad yelled, "Nisay! Over here." He glanced at Francie and me and explained. "That's the Cambodian man and his family we've been helping get settled. Laney and I took them some things this morning. Come say hello."

Walking toward us were a small man and woman, and four children ranging in sizes from around my age to first-graders, all holding hands. Every one of them had a look on their faces like they were afraid they were going to be kicked, and they seemed to cower under our attention.

The oldest boy looked to be about my age. He was my height and skinny. He probably weighed even less than I did. I might have seen him at school, but he flitted around the edges of the classrooms like he was always in hiding. Tonight, he appeared to be wearing three or four shirts of different sizes, but even so, I could see that he was shivering.

Nisay introduced his wife and children to us. I could barely understand his strongly accented English, but I nodded politely. He grabbed Francie's dad's hand and pumped it. "Thank you, Mr. Ivey, for the food you brought. We had nice meal. And thank you for the clothes. They are very helpful."

I could hardly breathe. I had taken this jacket, even though I had a winter coat, merely because I wanted it. I didn't really need it, despite the fact that I had convinced myself I did. But this boy, whatever his name was, needed it for real.

I thought about Francie's mom telling me I could make my own choices, and I realized, if I were going to be different from my dad, I needed to make a different choice than the one I had made earlier in the day. The world wasn't all about me and my ideas of what I needed to feel accepted.

Understanding what had to be done, I rubbed my hand one more time down the sleeve of the jacket I loved. I knew I would remember the feel of the soft cloth on my skin for a long time. Then I slowly unzipped the jacket, pulled it off, and handed it to the boy. He gave me a questioning look. I gestured that it was his and he should put it on. He did. A smile filled his face. That coat must have been warm from my body heat as well as from its padding.

Nobody spoke for what seemed like a long while. Finally, the boy's dad said, "Thank you, little miss." They all bowed a little and moved on. "Happy Christmas," he called over his shoulder.

"That was nice of you, Faye," said Laney. "But now we should get you home before you freeze to death." Francie squeezed my hand but said nothing. We turned toward the car.

Strangely, I didn't feel the least bit cold as I walked to the car. I had made my own choice. I wasn't my dad. And I understood how great Santa probably felt when he handed out gifts.

Other things happened in the next few months that would change my life. But that's another story I'll save for another time. I just want you to know that that Christmas was the most magical one I can ever remember. I never regretted giving up that jacket.

It was just a jacket, after all.

Faye isn't particularly close to the edge in this short story, mostly because it's Christmas, and she loves this time of year. She is the main character in my novel, Who She Is, and she comes extremely close to her personal edge several times. Faye wants to run the Boston Marathon, but it's 1967 and women aren't allowed. Besides, her parents won't let her do it. Regardless, she practices in secret and is determined to find a way. While she's running, she starts having flashbacks of a different early life and different parents. Her mom says the flashbacks aren't real but are related to her epilepsy, but Faye isn't sure. She starts an investigation that will change her life completely, and only her determination to find the truth and her willingness to tiptoe to her personal edge will save her.

This story was first published <u>Tangled Lights and Silent Nights: A Holiday Anthology</u>. 2018.

RIVER MAGIC

We put in near Blue Spring State Park, which is a manatee refuge on the St. John's River in Central Florida. I settle onto my Wilderness ten-foot-long kayak that fits me like an extension of my own body. My husband climbs into his considerably larger Hobie, which allows him to pedal as well as paddle. He's planning on fishing while I observe nature and hope to see a manatee.

But it's late March, one of the first hot, muggy days of the season. The thousand-pound manatees that spend the winters gliding just under the river's surface have probably already made their way out to the colder waters of the ocean. I wouldn't blame them. But this is the first afternoon I've been able to take away from work in months, so I am hopeful but not optimistic.

It's the way I feel about my marriage.

Every year, my husband and I run away from our problems and spend the winter in our retirement haven, a double-wide trailer perched beside a beautiful lake in Central Florida. We've always had our best times on vacation, and this feels like a four-months-long vacation. That is, until we begin to think about going back to our real lives. And then the weight of our upcoming return to reality makes us both cranky.

We are hoping for a good day, a reminder of why we are together. So we paddle upstream first, planning to drift back downstream when we are tired. A short way upstream is the run to Blue Spring. The water's year-round seventy-three degrees lures manatees in the colder months, and tubers and swimmers the rest of the year. We slide over a rope stretched across the entrance and glance at a sign that warns away fishermen and motorboats. My husband pulls in his fishing line and we paddle in to explore.

On the way to the spring, the water is deep and clear, like a natural aquarium. Some of the fish swimming beneath our kayaks are five feet long or more, with pointed noses. Gar, I think they're called. Others look more like regular fish, with rounded noses. These might be mullet. But I see no manatees, and neither have any of the tourists strolling along the boardwalk beside the stream. The day isn't over, though.

We return to the river and my husband lets out his fishing line again. The current is just strong enough to require us to paddle every few seconds if we want to get anywhere. But there's no place to go, really. The banks and as far as we can see are covered with trees and brush in myriad colors of green. I recognize palm trees, of course, and cypress and oaks, but nothing else. I paddle haphazardly and try to stay out of the way of the rental boats and tandem kayaks that race by me. Signs posted on tree trunks warn boaters to make no wake, because this is a manatee zone. Except that it isn't, at least not on this day. Maybe the drivers of the boats don't notice the signs.

We turn off onto a branch, a loop that my husband has seen on his phone's GPS. The other kayaks and motorboats don't bother, so we have the place to ourselves. He wants to stop and fish, so I rest my paddle across my legs. I spend the next half hour trying to describe the color of the new leaves on the cypress trees. I don't come up with much. Spring green. Shamrock green. The green of a shiny new traffic light. None of these pitiful attempts comes close to describing the vibrant color, but it does describe my thinking: slow and relaxed, like the rest of me. I don't particularly care whether I capture the best description for the green. I'm happy just to be noticing.

Eventually, my husband gives up on fishing and we paddle onward, through a narrowing stream in a forest that could easily harbor Tarzan, or a Bigfoot of the swamp. As a child, one of my favorite television shows was about a ranger who drove an airboat through the Everglades. It could have been filmed here, I think, instead of the real Everglades. I can still hum the theme song. Or is that a different song altogether? I can't remember, and it doesn't matter right now. Unfortunately, Florida has changed since I was a child. The state's natural resources are threatened by pollution, unfettered growth, and global warming. I choose not to worry about those problems today.

Great blue herons stand upright and still as they watch for just the right dinner to swim their way, and then strike in an instant to come up with a wriggling fish. Snake-birds pop their long black necks up from the water and swim for a moment before diving back down. Snowy egrets with question-mark necks fly over. I don't spot any alligators, but I hear their grunts deep in the lily pads. It's mating season, so maybe they are calling for a partner. Or warning me off. My feet are dangling over the edge of the kayak. I make a point to pull them in, safeguard my toes. I've never heard of an alligator bothering a kayaker, but a little caution seems an appropriate response.

On this perfect spring day, a few clouds make for fun watching but don't portend any rain. The wind blows just strongly enough to keep away the mosquitoes. Deep, dark, nearly still water carries me along. There is not a single thing I need to do right now. My bug spray and sunscreen do their work, and my water bottle is within easy reach. I resonate with Huck and Jim, dozing and drifting down the river.

Eventually the loop brings us back to the main river. I'm a bit sorry to return to civilization, or at least to what passes for it on the river. Pre-teen boys pilot their family's rent-a-boat with smug smiles, and drunk men swill beer as they race through the no-wake zones. It is a typical day on the water.

As we drift toward our take-out place, I can't predict how the next months will go, or whether my husband and I will be able to live with our intractable problems, much less overcome them. I can't foresee the future. I just know we both enjoy being on the water, and I'll take this sweet memory back into the real world.

I'm sorry, but not surprised, that I didn't see any manatees on this day. I hope to try again next year, when the cool days and relatively warm spring water invite the giant sea creatures to tarry a while. I'm hopeful, but not optimistic, that my husband and I will make it back here to see them.

No matter how close we are to the edge, a nice day will often return us to safe footing. Sometimes, that's all it takes.

This essay was first published in <u>Nature's Healing Spirit:</u> <u>Real Life Stories to Nurture the Soul,</u> by Sheri McGregor. 2018. San Marcos, CA: Sowing Creek Press.

WHEN IT'S YOUR TIME

June

Arnie

We took Clara to the doctor today for a check-up because she's been coughing a lot. They did a chest x-ray, and it showed a spot. The doctor says it could be lots of stuff: TB, an infection, or cancer. He'll do a biopsy next week. She stopped smoking ten years ago, so I'm sure it's nothing bad. We got our favorite lunch while we were out, conch fritters and fries. Man, I love those things. Well, we're back and there's still some light left. I think I'll mow the lawn.

Sherry

Mom called me this afternoon to tell me she has lung cancer! They found a spot on her lungs and tests showed it was cancer. I was afraid it would happen sometime. All those cigarettes. What was it, about three packs a day? I didn't want to ask when she called, and I don't guess it matters now. I wonder what happens next. I hate to think this way, but I can't help wondering how much time from work this is going to cost me. It's hard to be the director of a management consulting company and take a lot of time off work to deal with my parents' issues. I'll do what I can, but I'm a thousand miles away.

I wonder if she gave us all lung cancer with her second-hand smoke. I'm glad I refused to let her smoke around Laurie when we visited. At least my daughter and her baby-to-be ought to be all right. Should I get a chest x-ray, like Mom suggested?

She cried on the phone when she told me the news. I can't remember her doing that before. Dad was off doing something else when she called. Why wasn't he with her? *Duh.* When was he ever with her when something intense was happening? Poor Mom. I hope she makes it through this, but I bet she won't. What will I do without her? She knows all those "soft" things that I never could get the hang of. Who will I call when I spill cranberry juice on my best white blouse? And I need to get her recipe for that hamburger and cornmeal stuff she makes that's so good.

Oh, man, this could be really bad! I wonder how Joe took it.

Joe

I was at the hospital yesterday with Mom and Dad when we got the diagnosis. They don't know what kind of cancer it is yet. Mom looked pretty bad, and boy was she loopy. She kept looking for her glasses, and they were on her nose all the time. And she kept losing her worry beads. What in the hell are those things? She's not Catholic. But they did seem to keep her hands busy.

I looked up lung cancer on the web last night. There are several kinds, and some of them aren't so bad. I bet it's one of the easier kinds, and the treatment will be successful. I'm not going to get too upset at this point.

I don't know what to say to Sam about all this. What do you tell a six-year-old about cancer? He loves going to Grandma's house after school. She plays games and reads to him, and she nearly always has supper ready for us when I pick him up.

Look on the bright side, I always say.

July

Sherry

The cancer is the bad kind. Not the worst, though. Unfortunately, because it's in both lungs, surgery isn't an option. Mom cries every time I call her. I don't know what to say. "There, there, it'll be all right"? I don't think that's true. "I'm so sorry, Mom," is about all I can say. I don't feel right saying, "You don't deserve this," because maybe she does. It's what smoking does to a person. And my brother still smokes. How could he?

Mom wants me there when she visits the oncologist for the first time. I'd like that, too. Dad will probably find some excuse not to go, so maybe Joe will go with us. But he's so busy in the shoe store that he might not have time. I guess it's up to me, even though I'll have to fly down there the day of the appointment and then fly back the next day. Can I reschedule that big training program that's set for the same day? Probably not. Maybe Fred can coordinate it for me. I'm doing my best to be available for everyone who needs me, but I feel overwhelmed.

The plane fares from Washington to Tampa are that

high? *Whew*. Don't the airlines give breaks for family emergencies? Oh, yeah, that fare–that $600 one, that's for a family emergency. I could get it for half price if I could wait two weeks. *Yeah, right*. I need to be at the oncology meeting.

Arnie

Where is that cancer insurance policy we bought years ago? It'll come in handy now. There it is in the top drawer. Good thing I handle things like this. Clara never was any good at practical things. Always painting her pictures that we have to find room for on the walls, or visiting some shut-in. Or putting her nose in a book. I bet she doesn't know a thing about the state of our finances.

My arthritis is acting up, and my hip is killing me. I've been taking Clara to so many doctor appointments that I haven't had time to schedule my own. She usually keeps the schedules for those sorts of things, but she forgot to take care of my checkup. I guess she was distracted, but I'm feeling pretty ignored here. Got to get over that, though. She needs me now.

I'll be glad when Sherry arrives, so she can take Clara to her doctor appointments. I need to get to the shoe store more often. Joe's a good manager, but I have to stay on top of him. He doesn't keep the books the way I like, and he hasn't been ordering far enough in advance. Shoe styles change all the time, he says, so he likes to wait to see what's coming up. I think he's just lazy. Stock the old faithful shoes, I insist, but he wants to "innovate." He's going to run that store into the ground if I don't stay on him every minute. And now, with Clara sick, we're really going to need the money. What a load of worries.

Sherry

That doctor's appointment was exhausting. Seeing those poor people hooked up to their chemo machines, knowing that in a few months, most of them will be dead, just did me in. They looked so hopeful. So did Mom. That was what affected me the most. I had a hard time holding back my tears.

Her doctor decided to do a set of radiation treatments and a few months of chemo, every week if Mom can stand it. One good thing is that her hair won't fall out. That meant a lot to me, but Mom didn't seem to care. She's just eager to get started.

Mom chose to stay in the waiting room while I spoke with the oncologist alone. She probably knew what I was going to ask him, but I guess she didn't want to know the answer. I didn't either, really, but I need to plan. He says she has somewhat less than a year to live, less if the treatment doesn't work. Her passing could be easy or hard, with anxiety and breathing problems. If the cancer goes to her brain, she could develop dementia. But, he said, some people do well with the treatment and live a lot longer than expected. In terms of talking to Mom about it, he'll take his cue from her. If she wants to talk about dying, he will, but otherwise he'll assume she doesn't want to know.

When I came out of his office, Mom didn't ask what he'd said, so I didn't tell her. I'm following his lead. For now, we'll focus on the treatment and hope it works.

She looks scared, but otherwise okay. She's kind of low on energy and seems a little depressed, but who wouldn't? I'm glad I could be there for her. She kept squeezing my hand when the doctor talked to us, and she thanked me over and over for coming with her.

As soon as we got home, she went to report to her prayer group. That woman sure has a lot of people praying for her. Bless them all.

How am I going to manage this? I live so far away and have a demanding job. If I take a leave of absence for the next year, I'm afraid my job won't be there when I return. Besides, I don't have that kind of money saved. For now, I'll just have to fly back and forth and trust that Joe will call me when I'm needed.

Joe

Sherry isn't around much, so she thinks everything is going well enough. But I see what's really going on because I'm over there every day. Mom and Dad stay in different rooms and don't have much to do with each other. She reads the Bible and he watches television. I don't know how to talk about the situation with them, so I try to be cheerful and help out when I can. But the whole thing is really sad.

The doctor told Sherry that Mom might last a lot longer than he thinks. That's what I'm banking on. Lots can happen in a year. Maybe they'll even find a cure.

August

Arnie

I hate taking Clara to chemo, though I don't say so. Looking at those poor doomed souls makes me want to cry. I don't stay with her, because it takes a while. I go grocery shopping instead. Shopping isn't so bad. I can buy most of the same stuff Clara bought and still save about twenty dollars. She doesn't like that I buy different brands, but we need to save all the money we can. Even with Medicare and a cancer policy, this treatment is going to be long and expensive.

Funny, she doesn't seem to mind the chemo. She's always happy to see the people there. It's like they're buddies. They chatter away about their treatments. Lots of talk about their appetites. Clara's always had a good appetite, and she still does. She's a little tired the day or two after the chemo, but then she bounces back. She still goes to water aerobics when she can, and we walk every morning that she feels like it.

I miss my companion, though. She talks on the phone all the time to her prayer group and her friends. She hardly ever talks to me.

Joe

Mom hasn't been interested in cooking for a while, so I go over every night now and prepare supper. She still watches Sam after school, but she doesn't color with him much anymore. Mostly they watch videos or she sends him outside to play basketball with the kids next door.

I don't mind cooking. The food Dad gets is weird, though, so I use my own ingredients. He's gotten really cheap recently, and so critical of me. For example, he always criticizes what I cook. I'd like to see him fix a meal, even once. He doesn't know how to boil water. But Mom likes my cooking, and most nights she cleans her plate. I suspect she's never been waited on before.

I'm not sure how the treatments are going. Dad insists on taking her, which is fine by me. Sherry calls pretty often, and I gather she's working hard so she can get some time off and come for a week or two instead of just a few days.

October

Arnie

Clara hardly ever goes anywhere now. Her doctor doesn't want her to catch a virus from crowded places, and she's so tired that it would be hard for her to get out, anyway. She goes to Sunday School sometimes, where her friends pray over her. She always comes home happier.

I try to be helpful, but I don't have a lot of time, because I'm having to take care of the house now. I've learned how to iron, fix breakfast and lunch, and do the laundry. I do a pretty good job, if I say so myself. Not as good as Clara, of course.

God, will you give her one more year? Will you keep her healthy so she can celebrate her seventy-fifth birthday in March? I don't know why that date means so much to me. Probably it's because I didn't want to have a big party for our fiftieth anniversary. But if she makes it to her birthday, I'm going to throw her a huge party.

I made a boo-boo the other day. I asked Clara if she wanted to go and look at burial plots. She started crying and ran into the bathroom, and she didn't come out for an hour. I tried to apologize, but she didn't want to hear it.

November

Joe

Mom finished the chemo and radiation, but she's failing—I can see it. She keeps a smile plastered on her face and always tries to be optimistic. I wonder what she's really thinking. She doesn't talk to me about her feelings or concerns, and neither does Dad. Truthfully, I wouldn't know what to say if they did. I'm better at doing than talking.

I have to call Sherry and get her back down here. Mom needs help with the house. She's organized all the pictures, tidied her drawers, and washed the bedspreads, but the place hasn't been vacuumed in months. Whenever I go over there, she's lying on the couch, staring out the window. I don't think she even goes to church now. She and Dad watch some television pastor every Sunday morning.

The doctor brought in hospice this past week. Mom seemed relieved. The nurses come out a couple of times a week, and they'll come more often if we need them. But it's such a final move. The hospice people got her a wheelchair, and Dad and I have learned how to put her into it. I wheel her to supper every night, but she doesn't eat much now, and doesn't say much. One time she told me that she misses her mother, even though she's been gone for twenty-five years. All I could say was "I'm sorry, Mom." Her sisters call a lot, though. That's something.

Dad spends hours every day sitting with Mom now. As a matter of fact, he won't leave her alone, even for an instant. I overheard them talking about the "old days," when they first met. It's pretty sweet. I guess they were in love once, before us kids and the store came along.

After fifteen years together, Melissa has left me. A separation, she says. She complains that I'm never home and I don't pay any attention to her when I am home. I'm just like my dad, she says. Maybe she's right. But how can

I do better when I've got to cook for Mom and Dad every night and Melissa won't come with me? *Damn.* In a way, I'm relieved not to have to go home to that angry, disappointed silence every night. What a bitch to leave me now.

At least she left Sam with me. He cries at the least little thing, and I'm not sure how to help. It's all I can do to get him fed and to school on time. Unfortunately, I don't think I can leave him with Mom any longer. She's too weak. I'll find out about after-school care. Hopefully, he'll have friends there.

I have to keep the store profitable, because everybody depends on me. It's a good thing I have Carol as assistant manager. She's a lot nicer than Melissa.

Arnie

Clara's doctor told us about a drug trial she might qualify for. There's a new lung cancer drug that sometimes creates miracle cures. I'll do whatever it takes to get her in this study. It's an hour's drive away, but I don't care. Lord, just save her. I'll be a better husband. I'll pay more attention to her. I can't believe how I've taken our marriage for granted. She has been my rock for fifty-three years. The doctor says the side effects might be pretty bad, but we'll know within a month if the drug is going to work. Clara is willing, but the hospice nurse isn't very enthusiastic. I guess if Clara improves, she'll lose a patient. *Ha!*

Sherry

I've arranged to stay with my parents for the entire Thanksgiving week. Mom's sisters are coming to visit, too, and we'll cook Thanksgiving dinner together. It'll be the first time in more than fifty years that Mom won't have to cook. She says she won't mind letting that go. She just wants to spend time with her family.

Mom talks a lot about Beth, the hospice nurse. Apparently, Beth listens to her and will talk about anything. I gather Mom talks to her about dying, which she won't—or can't—do with us. I almost got my feelings hurt when I heard that, but I decided not to bother. It's all about Mom now, not me and my feelings. I'm just happy she has someone she likes to talk to.

December

Sherry

I took a couple of weeks off from work before Christmas. Mom is very weak, and she needs me. I have to take her to the bathroom and lift her onto the potty, then back into the wheelchair. This happens many times a day, because the experimental medicine gives her terrible diarrhea. I feel so sorry for her, especially those times when she doesn't make it. I have to clean her up, and that's deeply embarrassing for both of us. She cries and cries.

Our best times are when we just sit together. I knit, and she attempts to crochet. Her afghan doesn't get any bigger, but we don't mention it. I feel close to Mom, even though we don't say much. I'm glad she's stopped asking me when I'm getting married again. Dad and I take turns being on call at night, and we have to give her medicine every four hours. The morphine helps her breathing. For Christmas, I'm writing her a letter thanking her for all the things she's done for me. What could she possibly need now?

I asked her once if she was ready to give up and go. She got upset and said, "No, I'm not ready to leave my family." I didn't know how to respond. She's going to leave us, whether she's ready or not. Seems to me she would be better served to get her affairs in order and say goodbye to people, but it's not for me to say.

John calls nearly every night. I wasn't interested in getting serious with him before this trip, but now his calls are a lifeline. Also, I have to go outside for a walk every day. Dad doesn't like for me to leave her, but I would go crazy being inside all day every day. Mom doesn't even want to go out in the yard any more. I open the blinds for her, and she stares out the window.

Thank God for Joe. We're closer now than we've ever been. I can't believe Melissa left him. But that marriage has been bad for years. Carol seems a better fit. I don't think they have anything going except a friendship, but she gives him support. He's over here every night, cooking supper and doing whatever is needed. It would be fun to go out dancing together if we're not too tired. But who am I kidding? That won't happen anytime soon.

Dad loses it sometimes, and yells at us. We don't wash the dishes right. We leave stuff out that should be put away. We spend too much money. The other night he really lost it: started screaming when Mom accidentally knocked over her water glass. I talked to the hospice nurse, and she called the social worker. He was calmer after the two of them talked.

Arnie

Christmas wasn't going to be much this year. We decided not to buy presents or put up a tree. Taking care of Clara takes too much out of us, and nobody felt like celebrating. But the most amazing thing happened on Christmas Eve. We were all together, trying to watch "Miracle on 34th Street," when the doorbell rang. I got up to answer it, and it was Clara's Sunday School class, six ladies who trooped in and brought us Christmas dinner. Clara's face lit up, and tears came to my eyes. They sang some Christmas carols, and we all joined in. It was hard singing through the tears. We had the greatest Christmas dinner ever, I think. Even Clara ate a little.

I thought everybody had forgotten about us. I won't forget this Christmas—it may be the last one we're all together.

Joe

Christmas was so sad. Melissa had Sam on Christmas Day, so I spent the day with the P's. I remember when I was little and they would put our toys under the tree before they went to bed. I woke up really early to see what was there and then went back to bed, and only got up when Mom called me to breakfast. We'd eat and then open presents, and I'd play with mine all day. Boy, I'd give a lot to have one of those uncomplicated Christmases again.

January

Arnie

We had to give up on the experimental drug, because it made Clara too sick. I guess that was why the hospice nurse wasn't excited about it. She said nobody she knows has done well on it. So that's it. What will I do without her? My arthritis is acting up so bad, most nights I don't even try to sleep. I just sit beside Clara's bed and drift off. I can't keep it up, though, because I'm no good to anybody. But I have to be there for Clara. It doesn't matter about my pain. I can care for myself later. How can I thank her for the many years we've had? Maybe a miracle will happen. I can't give up hope, because Clara hasn't.

Sherry

I had to take a leave of absence from work. I was too exhausted and emotionally drained to keep going back and forth. So, I'm here for the duration. We've got to hire a private duty nurse, though. I can't stay up with her every night, even if Dad can.

The hospice nurse is here once a day now, and more often when we need her. I can't believe any person can be so nice. She has an assistant who bathes Mom and cleans the house, which gives me a break. Mom perks up when they come.

The cancer has spread to her brain. I can't say for sure, but she seems to spend a lot of time back on the North Carolina farm of her girlhood, and she thinks I'm her younger sister. Yesterday she had the happiest look on her face when she pointed out the angels in the room to me. I had to go into my bedroom and cry for a while after that incident.

In her lucid moments, which are less and less frequent, she gives me stuff—her furs and her engagement ring, because it falls off her finger now. She told me what she wants to be buried in, and what songs she wants played at her funeral. I try to be calm and matter-of-fact when she does these things, but my heart breaks. On the other hand, all of our suffering will be over when she's gone. Oh, no. I can't believe I even thought such a thing.

February

Arnie

They took Clara to the hospice facility today. She couldn't breathe, so I called the nurse. She came right away and said, "It's time. Let's get her to the residential center." I followed the ambulance in the car. Sherry had gone to the beach for a couple of days. She was just too worn out to do much, she said. It seemed pretty selfish to me, and I told her so. I don't care if she did get a lady to come and stay with Clara in her place or that she came right back when I called. It wasn't right for her to leave. I don't take a break.

The hospice is exceptionally nice. It's too bad Clara can't see how beautiful it is, or how nice the staff people are. They say she's in a coma, but sometimes she comes out of it a little and mumbles something. The last time she came out, I told her I loved her and would be okay if she was ready to leave. I wonder if it's true.

The kids will be here soon. The nurse told us to pay our last respects.

Joe

I had just come home from the hospice house when they called and said Mom was gone. It was an easy passing, they said. I had waited with her for hours, but she kept breathing those painful, syrupy breaths. I had to go to work, so I left. Dad was in the bathroom and Sherry had gone to get a cup of coffee. When she came back into the room, Mom was just lying there peacefully. The hospice people say it often happens that way. I guess it's easier to leave when your loved ones aren't holding you back. I threw my cigarettes away after I heard the news. I'm done with them. It was all I could do for Mom now.

Sherry

In a way, I can't believe Mom is gone. In another way, I'm happy she's no longer struggling to breathe. Those last weeks were brutal for all of us. I think she would have liked the funeral, though. People overflowed the chapel and sang her favorite songs, and the pastor talked about what a good woman she was. We buried her in a pretty cemetery plot that she'd chosen. Dad will be beside her when his time comes. Family arrived from everywhere: sisters, grand-children, even my newborn granddaughter who Mom never got to see. And, whew, the friends that woman made in her seventy-four years on earth. I hope to be so loved.

March

Joe

I wish Mom had been here for Sam's seventh birth-day party. She would have been so happy to celebrate with us. We put her picture on the table beside the cake and told Sam she was watching him from heaven. He seemed happy with that.

Melissa and I filed for divorce. We'll work out joint custody. It's a huge blow for Sam, especially since he just lost his grandma, but he'll get through it. I think Carol and I may have a chance. We see each other every day at work, and that makes me happy. Sam likes her, too.

Dad is talking about going on a cruise—to rest, he says. He can't bear to be in the house alone, and it's too quiet for him to sleep. Hospice has a grief program that he'll attend. I talk to him every day, real talk about our feelings, and he's kinder than before. He's also working things out so I can buy the store on good terms. He says he's tired of it. He's got some buddies who get together and play golf and fish. I still cook for him every night, because it gives me a chance to see him. Maybe he can move in with Sam and me for a while.

Arnie

I've got to go to the doctor and see about this arthritis. Now, unfortunately, I've got all the time in the world. This house is too lonely for me. I try to be out of it as much as possible. Even though the hospice people say not to make any big decisions right away, I'll probably move when I can face it. Or I'll go and stay with my sister. She lost her husband a few years ago, so she knows what it's like. My world is completely empty without Clara. At least I did the best I could during her last months, even if I didn't always. I hope I made up for some of my neglect.

Sherry

I miss my mom so much it hurts. Still, I treasure the time we spent together at the end. I'm so glad I could be there for her when she needed me most. Losing her has made me reassess my priorities. I don't think I'll return to my job. It doesn't seem as important as before all this happened. I'm tired of working sixty hours a week, and I need a break. I have enough money saved to last a few months, and then I'll figure out what to do next. Maybe I'll go back to school. Life is too precious to waste it at a job I don't love.

John asked me to travel with him to Hawaii, and I think I will.

The Next December

Arnie

I know it's early, but I'm too old to delay getting married. My kids think I should wait for at least a year, so I will, but that's only a couple of months away. I'm not sure they approve that I found somebody so soon, but I'm ready to start a new life. Suzanne is not Clara, but she's a good companion, and I love her. Both of my kids are getting married in the next year, too.

I hope Clara is looking down on us and smiling. I think she is.

I wrote this not too long after my mother died of lung cancer. Her name was Ruth, not Clara, and she wasn't the character in this story. Neither were the rest of us. The wonderful thing about fiction is that you can keep the deeper truth of a situation without getting mired in the details. I changed much about the story, including names and circumstances. What I kept was the way one person's struggle is reflected in the lives of her family members. The family's determination to support Clara's journey transforms them in ways no one could have predicted. They stepped off the cliff and found their lives to be richer, deeper, and more honest on the other side.

AUTHOR'S NOTE

Thank you for reading my short story compilation. I hope you've enjoyed it. If you want to read more of my writing, please check out my website: www.dianebyington.com, and sign up for my newsletter. I'll let you know when new stories and books will be published.

Also, I'd love it if you picked up one of my novels, *Who She Is* or *If She Had Stayed.* The first chapters of the books are reproduced in the following pages.

Please let me know if you liked this little book. And stay in touch. You can contact me at www.dianebyington.com/contact.

And stay away from that edge!!!

WHO SHE IS

Red Adept Publishing, 2018

Chapter 1

October 4, 1967

MY FIRST DAY at Valencia High started with a bloody nose. I had physical education class right after homeroom, and I wandered around the sprawling school, looking for the gym, for ten minutes. When I finally found it and changed into my PE uniform, I saw that the other girls were playing volleyball. I groaned. I loved nearly all sports, but I had always loathed volleyball. Something about spiking the ball and charging the net never worked for me. But of course, I didn't have a choice. The teacher assigned me to a group with another white girl and two black girls, who eyed me with suspicion. That kind of thing happened in every school. I was the perpetual new girl, the one nobody trusted.

Sure enough, as soon as we started playing, one of

the black girls elbowed me in the nose. Immediately, blood spurted all over my clothes. I lay on the floor and tried not to cry. The girl apologized and helped me up, and the teacher gave me a towel to hold over my nose. She told the white girl from my team to take me to the nurse's clinic.

"Thanks," I said to the girl when we were on our way. "I don't
think I could have found the clinic on my own."

"Sure. Not a problem. I hate volleyball."

I glanced at her to see if she'd read my mind and was making fun of me, but she seemed serious. I tried to remember her name, but pain and embarrassment drove out that information.

"Me, too," I said, sniffing back blood. "It's my first day here."

"Not a great way to start at a new school. But your mom will probably come and take you home or at least bring you clean clothes."

"Not likely."

"Really? Why not?"

I sighed. There was no way I was going to get into my family's weirdness with a girl whose name I couldn't even remember. I held the towel more tightly on my nose and mumbled from beneath it,
"She's really busy."

"That's too bad. Your nose isn't great."

That was cold comfort, but I nodded, trying to be polite.

She guided me through a maze of hallways to a door marked Nurse's Clinic. Smiling, she said, "See you around," before turning away.

⊙❀☙

UNSURPRISINGLY, MOM said she was too busy to come

to the school. Luckily, the nurse helped me clean myself up enough to attend the rest of my classes. My nose looked like a balloon and felt like a hammer was pounding into it, but I held my head down and tried to cover my face with my hair.

Just before the end of the last class, the principal gave announcements for the next day over the intercom. I listened with half an ear and thought about my crummy life. Moving all the time, new schools every few months, walking into classrooms and having everyone stare at me—I could go on and on about my woes, but it did absolutely no good. Nobody cared how I felt.

"Should meet at the track tomorrow..."

Wait. Had the principal said something about the track team? I tapped the guy in front of me on the shoulder, and he turned to look at me. "What did he say about track?" I asked.

He glanced at my nose then quickly looked away. "They're looking for some new kids to be on the track team. Tryouts are tomorrow."

"Do they take girls?"

"I don't know. I guess so." He shrugged, nodded, and turned back around.

Suddenly, my nose didn't hurt so much. I loved to run. I ran around all the time on the farms where we lived, just for the fun of it. Being on the track team would give me something to do other than go right home after school and start on my chores. And it might also give me a life of my own, for however long it lasted.

THAT EVENING DURING supper, I gave it a shot. I hadn't asked to do anything after school since I'd played basketball in Ohio, two moves back, and Mom owed me this. Glancing between Mom and Dad, I said, "They're looking for new people on the track team. I'd like to try out. Mom, will you pick me up at four thirty tomorrow?"

She stared at me for a moment before saying, "After what happened to you today, you want to do something athletic? I can't believe you."

"It was just an elbow in the nose. I guess I got too close to that girl when she was trying to spike the ball. That won't happen when I'm running."

"It wasn't just an elbow in the nose. You could have fallen down and hit your head, and that might have triggered a seizure. You're too fragile to take risks like that. In fact, I'm going to write a note so that you won't have to take PE at all."

I fought the urge to roll my eyes. She only brought up my epilepsy when she didn't want me to do something. It never stopped her from making me do heavy work around the house, like washing windows or moving furniture. No matter what my mom said, I knew running wasn't bad for me, because I'd run long and hard playing basketball without the slightest problem.

Mom always kept me from doing what I wanted. I was tired of it. "But, Mom, I like PE, except for volleyball. I'll be more careful. Don't write a note. It'll make me stand out even more than I already do."

She bit her lip and glanced at Dad, who shrugged. Then she shook her head in defeat. "All right, I won't. This time. But if it happens again, I will write that note. Now, eat your supper."

I took a few bites and tried again. "I really want to try out for the track team. I'd play basketball if I could, but the gym teacher said they don't have a girls' team here. Besides, I haven't had a seizure for as long as I can remember."

"Which is exactly why you shouldn't join the track

team. Running is harder on your body than basketball, Faye. I don't want to risk it."

That made no sense. "You wouldn't be risking it. I would."

Dad slammed his hand on the table. "Don't sass your mother," he said, raising his voice and giving me a stern look.

Dad mostly ignored me, but things didn't go well when he paid attention.

I looked down at my food. "Sorry."

Arguing was getting me nowhere, so I needed to change my strategy. Mom got weird sometimes, and when that happened, lying was my best bet.

After I washed the dishes, I asked Mom, in my most innocent voice, if I could stay after school the next day and go to the library. "The math teacher's going to tutor people who need it, and I'm really behind." I tried to keep the sarcasm out of my voice when I continued. "It's not running, so it shouldn't harm me."

She grunted then folded and shook out the dish towel several times. "All right, you can do that as long as you keep your medicine with you."

I headed to my room and managed to maintain a straight face until I'd closed my bedroom door. Then the smile broke through. Success!

AFTER SCHOOL THE NEXT afternoon, I sat on the bleachers and watched as six boys in maroon-and-orange T-shirts ran around the track. A slim man in shorts stood on the infield grass, a whistle around his neck, tapping his foot. The coach, I presumed. He glanced at his watch and frowned. Eventually, a boy came out from the school and wandered over. After a short conversation, he joined the others on the track.

I waited, but nobody else showed. Finally, leaving my books on the bench, I made my way over to the coach. He was writing something on a clipboard but looked up when I stopped a few feet away. The eagerness in his eyes turned to disappointment when he saw me.

He asked in a strong accent, "Can I help you, young lady?"

I couldn't think of how to begin, so I just stood there, tongue nailed to the roof of my mouth. He tapped his foot and waited.

I cleared my throat and said in as strong a voice as I could muster,

"I'd like to try out for the track team."

The corners of his mouth twitched as he stared at me. "Back home in Cuba, girls were involved in all aspects of sports. But in Valencia, only boys are allowed to join the track team. I'm sorry. I wish I could help you, young lady, but I can't." He turned his attention back to his clipboard.

I stood rooted to my spot, getting more annoyed by the second. He obviously needed to add people to the team, and from what I could tell, only one new boy had shown up. After all I'd gone through to be there, the coach wouldn't even let me try out for the piddly high school track team just because I was a girl?

I cleared my throat. When he looked up again, I said, "Uh, how far is one lap around the track?"

"A quarter mile. Four laps make a mile." He smiled at me. "You can run for fun if you want to. Just stay in the outside lanes. But if

you're going to run, let me give you a tip: start slow."

I walked back to my seat and untied the wraparound skirt I'd worn to school over my shorts. I would run a mile that day if I had to crawl. And I would run it as fast as my feet would carry me.

I joined the boys and began to jog on the track's soft surface. The rubber gave a little with each step. I felt like I was running on a trampoline or a cloud. I stretched out my legs and swung my arms and watched the world whiz by. My mind settled into a peaceful hum, my breath slow and easy.

The first curve arrived quickly. I sped up. The jog turned into a flat-out sprint, with my feet kicking up high behind me and my arms pumping. As I ran, I lifted my arms out to shoulder height, feeling about three years old. I pretended to be an airplane, for no other reason than that it was fun, and laughed for sheer joy.

The boys on the track team glanced at me curiously, but nobody said anything, so I kept running. Some of them were faster than I was, but I didn't care. I was running like the wind, and I felt light and free.

Before long, the Central Florida heat and humidity got to me, and I started breathing faster. I slowed down just a little. Then I noticed that a girl had joined me on the track. She was running slowly, as though it hurt.

I caught up to her and matched her pace. "Hi, I'm Faye."

She looked at me and said in a snotty tone, "Yeah, I know. You told me when I took you to the clinic yesterday. In case you don't remember, I'm Francie."

I could feel my face flush. "I'm sorry I didn't recognize you. I was in a lot of pain yesterday." Because we moved so often, I had an ironclad rule to not make close friends so I wouldn't be sad or miss people when we moved. Mostly, I didn't even bother to learn people's names. Francie would just have to get over being mad. Or not. I really didn't care. Running was one of those things a person could do alone, and I was used to being alone.

I sprinted off and ran around the track as fast as I could. When I lapped her, I slowed down and waited for her to accept my apology. But she didn't even look at me. *All right, then.* I was done trying to make up.

But after half a lap of running at her pace and not talking, I couldn't help myself. "So, *Francie*, do you run a lot?" I knew I should follow the ironclad rule, but she was a girl, and she was out running. We didn't have to be friends to run together.

"Today's my first day. I read in a magazine about this girl who got attacked by the race director when she ran the Boston Marathon last spring. Can you believe that? It pissed me off so much I decided to try running."

The Boston Marathon. Something about it sounded familiar, but I couldn't place it. I shook my head and looked over at Francie. She seemed to be waiting for me to say something.

"So how do you like it? Running, I mean."

She panted as she said, "I'm not sure. It's harder than I thought it would be."

I didn't think running was hard. I liked the rhythm of my feet hitting the ground and the way the wind dried the sweat from my face. I wasn't sure what else to say, so I ran ahead, gradually speeding up until I was flying. After my fourth lap, I collapsed onto the grass, huffing and puffing. I'd run hard, and except for being tired, I felt fine. Mom had been wrong about running causing a seizure.

The coach walked over to me, a big smile on his face. "I timed you, and you were faster than most of the boys. You didn't tell me you were such a good runner."

I laughed. "You didn't ask. You just turned me down."

"I'm sorry about before. You know, I don't think the rules specifically exclude girls. I guess it's just a custom here. Anyway, I'd like to have you on the team. I can't say for sure, but you're fast enough that you might even get a track scholarship to college."

A track scholarship? Really? I couldn't keep the grin from my face.

Convincing him to change his mind about me hadn't been too hard. Maybe Mom would be just as easy to win over. I'd give it another try when I got home.

He leaned over to shake my hand. "I'm Coach Lopez. Welcome to the team."

Francie joined us, panting and flushed. Coach Lopez asked her if she wanted to be on the track team, too. "You're not fast, but I can tell you've got endurance. I can train you to go faster, and you might be good in the two-mile race."

"No, thanks. I do want to go far, but fast doesn't interest me."

"All right." He turned to me. "See you tomorrow after school." Glancing at Francie, he said, "I'll still coach you, if you want, even without you being on the team."

Francie shrugged and waved to me as she ran toward a woman who was standing in the doorway of the school. I picked up my books and headed for my locker. Not only had I made the team, but I might even get a scholarship to college. Suddenly, my world was bright with possibilities.

Then I spotted Mom walking toward me, an angry scowl pulling down the corners of her mouth. *Uh-oh. Trouble.*

I trudged to meet her, my mind spinning with thoughts of how I could get out of this situation.

Mom looked like a thundercloud. "You were supposed to be in the library," she said, spitting out the words like bullets.

"Uh, it turns out I got the day wrong. So I ran instead."

"I've been watching you for the last ten minutes, missy. You stayed after school to run, after I specifically told you not to last night."

She'd caught me, so I faced her and tried to keep the excitement out of my voice. "I wanted to try it, and I like it, Mom. I ran a mile today, and nothing bad happened. And I got on the track team."

Mom glanced around. The coach was staring at us as if he wanted to come over and introduce himself but was waiting for an invitation. Mom ignored him, took a deep breath, then turned to me and said in a low, tight voice, "Where are your books? We'll continue this when your father gets home."

⚜

WHEN MY DAD CAME IN from the orange groves, I heard Mom talking to him in a hushed voice. I tensed and waited for him to call me into the living room. Hopefully, he wouldn't be too mad.

"Faye, get in here." I winced at his tone. Apparently, he was.

When I went in, he was standing in the center of the room, an
angry scowl on his face. "I understand you lied to your mama."

"Well..." I sat down on the couch and crossed my legs, trying to keep the one on top from jiggling.

"What have we told you before about lying?" He wasn't yelling, at least not yet, but his words were clipped and careful, like he was holding himself back. I knew not to sass him when he sounded like that.

"That I shouldn't do it." Of course I knew it was wrong. But what choice did I have if I wanted to run?

His eyes bored into me. "That's right. So why did you?"

I stood up and faced him, quivering all over. "Because I feel like I can be good at running, and I'm not good at much else. You move me all over creation and expect me to be okay with it, but I'm not." In spite of my best effort, a whine crept into my voice. "Running doesn't hurt anybody. Why is it such a big deal?"

He took a breath and glanced toward Mom, who shook her head and marched into their bedroom, slamming the door behind her. Dad sighed and shrugged then went to the refrigerator and took out a bottle of Mountain Dew. After he took a drink, he said over his shoulder, "Go to your room. We'll let you know when you can come out."

I stomped to my room and turned the radio up loud. Aretha Franklin was belting out, "Respect," and I sang along as loudly as I dared.

Mom and Dad talked in their bedroom. I couldn't hear their words, but Mom sounded really upset. Eventually, Dad came out and called me back into the living room. In his most no-nonsense voice, he said, "Your mama thinks that even if other girls could run without harming themselves, which is doubtful, it's bad for your health. So you need to come home on the bus, and you can use your extra energy to weed Mr. Barrett's vegetable garden. You can only run on the track if it's during a class when you're supervised."

"But Coach Lopez will be..."

"I don't want to hear it. Maybe next time you'll think twice before you lie to your mama. Now, go and apologize to her."

I trudged to their closed bedroom door and called out, "Sorry. I won't do it again." Another lie. I would run again as soon as I could.

"All right," came the muffled voice from within. "Go do your homework."

⟨≫⟩

FOR A WEEK, I STAYED in my room as much as possible after school and barely made any headway in weeding the Barretts' vegetable garden. Ordinarily, I wouldn't have minded helping out the old people who owned the farm where we were tenants, but I was on strike, and I wanted it to show.

By Wednesday, I started to wonder if my strike was pointless. I had my heart set on being a PE teacher when I grew up. About the only thing I was good at was sports, so it made sense that I would be a good PE teacher. But to reach my goal, I would have to go to college. The truth was that farm workers like the people in my family didn't go to college. They started working in the fields as soon as they left high school and then worked until they dropped. Picking fruits and vegetables, all day every day, wasn't my idea of living. If my parents forced me to do that, I might as well be dead.

As I wallowed in my misery, I thought I must have been insane to even hope that I could accomplish something so... huge. The problem was that I didn't have another dream to replace that one. Still, a little voice deep inside told me that if I could do something big like get a scholarship to college, maybe I could make a different, happier future for myself.

By Friday, I'd decided that I wasn't quite ready to give up on this dream, even if it was pointless. Maybe a miracle would happen.

Only two and a half more years until I was eighteen, and then I would be free.

I've never been a runner, and I'm nowhere nearly as brave as Faye. I wanted to write a story about a girl who never gave up, who believed in herself, no matter how dire her situation or all the problems the world sent her way. She never went over that edge.

If you'd like to read the rest of **WHO SHE IS**, you can order it at any online retailer or ask your local bookstore to order it.

https://www.amazon.com/Who-She-Diane-Byington-ebook/dp/B079KGXB7W

IF SHE HAD STAYED

Red Adept Publishing, 2020

Chapter 1
"Time of the Season"

Struggling to keep her teeth from chattering, Kaley pushed on one of the back windows of the dilapidated Victorian home where Nikola Tesla had once lived. The hinge let out a loud squeak, and she froze. The houses were close together in that part of Colorado Springs, and a neighbor might call the police.

As the seconds ticked by, she considered what she should do if a police officer appeared around the corner of the old house. She was a fast runner, but no one could outrun a bullet. Fear flooded her chest, and her heart hammered, but uppermost in her mind was how embarrassed she would be if she had to call one of her friends to post bail for her.

After another long moment with no sign that she'd been caught, Kaley's heartbeat returned to normal. She'd come too far to stop. She placed a concrete block beneath the window, grabbed her flashlight and other tools, and hoisted herself over the sill.

A thrill ran up her spine. She'd never done anything illegal before, but she couldn't miss the opportunity to possibly discover something of Tesla's that no one else had found. She'd waited months for the previous tenant to move out, and the landlord had shown her the house that morning.

After looking around for a bit, she'd said, "Three thousand seems a little steep for this old neighborhood. Would you consider twenty-three hundred?" Even at that rate, she'd have to get roommates, which she was reluctant to do. She liked her privacy. Still, she would do it if she had to.

He laughed. "I just put up the sign yesterday, and five other people have already called to see it. I'm showing it to someone else in an hour if you don't want it."

She took a breath. "Has anybody found any Tesla artifacts here?"

"Not in the ten years that I've owned the house. If he'd left anything, it would have been snatched up years ago. Every single tenant asks about it, and I tell them all the same thing, but they think they'll discover something no one else has found." He shrugged. "Everybody's got a fantasy, you know?"

Kaley started to tell him she wasn't a dreamer but a historian, and she needed the artifacts for the Tesla museum she hoped to open, not for her own personal glory. Ultimately, she decided not to give him any more information about herself.

Tesla was known for hiding his inventions in places where his enemies, real or imagined, couldn't find them. Also, he preferred numbers that were divisible by three. Since his house number was 1533, it seemed like the perfect place to start her search.

Walking through the house with the landlord, she'd noticed that the window over the kitchen sink was open an inch, and a different plan started to form. "I'll have to think about it and call you back."

He shrugged. "Don't think too long."

When she called the landlord back in the afternoon, the house had been rented. The new tenant was planning to move in the next day, so she decided she had to break in that night.

She'd called Kevin, her boyfriend. They'd planned to drive up to Vail later that evening, spend the night in a fancy hotel, and ski their hearts out the next day—the last day of the ski season. "I'm so sorry, but I can't go with you tonight. I need to do something for work."

"Tonight? What could be that important? We've had this trip planned for weeks."

"See, I need to break into Tesla's old house and—"

"Whoa! You need to *break into* a house? For God's sake, why would you do that?"

She took a breath. "I know it sounds crazy, and I would never do something like this if it weren't necessary. The previous tenant moved out yesterday, and the new one will move in tomorrow, so it's my only chance to get in and search the house."

"It doesn't sound crazy—it *is* crazy. What are you looking for, anyway? I know it has to do with Tesla, but what, specifically?" He was starting to sound more than mildly annoyed.

"I-I'm not sure. Probably something to do with an undiscovered invention."

He was quiet for a long moment. She knew to give him time. He was lightning fast when doing karate, but he always chose his words carefully. It was one of her favorite things about him. He truly meant what he said.

"So you're telling me you want to break into this house and steal whatever you find. Is that right?"

"Not exactly."

"What, exactly?"

"I'd ask the owner if I could put it in the museum. It would bring in lots of visitors, and I'd get to—"

"Keep your job. Yeah, I know how that goes." He exhaled sharply. "I'm not going to get into an argument about this. You'll do what you want. But I've really been looking forward to this trip with you. There won't be another time to ski this season."

He was making things harder than necessary. Yes, skiing was fun, and she always enjoyed being with him. But the opportunity was too important to miss. "I'm sorry, sweetie. I just can't. Maybe I could come up tomorrow around lunchtime, after I get some sleep."

"No. That won't work. You'd miss most of the day, and I'd hang around waiting for you instead of skiing." Annoyance filled his tone. "Suit yourself, but I'm going without you. And don't call me if you get arrested." He ended the call.

She knew he got irritated when she put work above their plans, but she didn't do it often. She was willing to bet that he would be proud of her if—no, *when*—she found a new Tesla artifact, a treasure to share with the world. "I'm sorry, Kevin. I'll make it up to you," she'd said to the dead line.

Standing in the ancient kitchen, Kaley stood up and turned on her flashlight. She imagined Tesla walking through the rooms as he pondered an experiment with electricity or went to heat a kettle on the stove.

She started her search by methodically knocking on every wall to listen for any odd hollow places. When that didn't net anything, she paced every room on both floors, measuring from the walls in increments of three feet and tapping her foot to check for trapdoors.

Sometime in the middle of the night, she happened upon a loose floorboard in a secondfloor bedroom that was fifteen feet from the east wall and three feet from the south. Using her crowbar, she pried it up. Inside a small recess was a leather satchel like the ones doctors had used in the nineteenth century, with handles on top and a strap with a clasp. Holding her breath, she lifted it out, opened it, and shined her flashlight inside. The bag was filled with dusty newspapers. She gently removed them and laid them out on the floor.

The papers were all editions of the *Colorado Springs Gazette*, dated 1899 and 1900, which were the years Tesla had lived in the house. She took a deep breath and grinned. The landlord had been wrong. The previous tenants hadn't found everything. Moving carefully so as not to cause the old paper to crumble, she unfolded the earliest one. On the front page was an article titled "Mr. Tesla to Build Lab in Town."

She scanned the dozen newspapers and found that all of them had articles featuring Tesla in some way. The most intriguing article was "Tesla Fails to Appear for Speech at Inventors' Club." Apparently, Mr. Tesla had been missing for about a week at that time. He'd eventually turned up, so it hadn't become a major news story.

The only unusual things she discovered were a few handwritten letters in the margin of one of the newspapers. They didn't spell anything, though, even when she tried to treat them as an anagram.

Sitting back on her heels, she considered what she'd found. As exciting as it was to come across something new, the newspapers were not a major discovery. The articles were accessible to anyone who cared to check the *Gazette*'s archives. There was no way to know how the papers had gotten into the satchel or whether they had been put there by Tesla or someone else. She decided to take them with her and display them in the museum when it opened, even though they wouldn't be much of a draw.

Figuring that if previous tenants had overlooked one thing, there might be more, she hammered the floorboard back down and continued searching. When she heard birds announcing the approaching dawn, she had to admit defeat. She had wasted a perfectly good ski trip for very little gain.

Holding the satchel and her tools, she climbed out the kitchen window and gently closed it behind her. She would have to consider whether it was worth telling the landlord about the newspapers. Probably not. Many old houses contained vintage newspapers, and nobody cared.

* * *

The next evening, after a long nap and a good workout, she called Kevin. To her surprise, he answered on the first ring. He even seemed happy to hear from her.

She did her best to sound upbeat. "How was the skiing?"

He sighed. "It was okay. It would've been better with you, though. How was the breaking and entering?"

"Not great. I didn't find anything worthwhile, just some old newspapers." When he didn't respond, she continued. "I'm really sorry I didn't go with you. The whole thing was a bust. I missed spending the time with you."

A long moment later, he said, "Well, that's good, I

guess."

In spite of his hesitation, the call was going better than she could have hoped. "Would you like to come over tonight? I could give you a nice massage."

"No." After a pause, he said, "But you could come over here. I'm showered and ready for bed, and you could snuggle with me."

"Sure. I'll be right there." She breathed a sigh of relief. She had pulled that one out, apparently.

This novel is about regrets. Kaley had a major regret: leaving her boyfriend Scott while they were in college. There were reasons that she did and excellent reasons that she regretted it, but she struggled to move on from that mistake. When the opportunity to travel back in time and make a different decision presented itself, she took it. And she stayed right on the very edge for the entire trip.

If you'd like to read the rest of *If She Had Stayed*, you can order it at any online retailer or ask your local bookstore to order it.

https://www.amazon.com/She-Had-Stayed-Diane-Byington-ebook/dp/B084D619KF

ACKNOWLEDGEMENTS

I've had the fiction bug since I was in the fifth grade and re-wrote part of Great Expectations, by Charles Dickens, into contemporary language for an assignment. It was great fun, and it earned me an A. So, thank you to that English teacher, whose name I don't remember.

Although I fantasized about writing fiction for many years, I didn't do much about it until ten years ago, when I decided to get serious about my goal. These stories span the past ten years of my writing journey. All but one of them was published in literary journals or anthologies, and getting those (rare) acceptance letters gave me enough confidence to continue working on my craft. So, thank you, journal editors.

My critique group, Tall Pines Fiction Writers, read these stories and helped me fashion them. Thanks to Rachel Craft, Jenn Perez, Josh Pollock, Heather Starsong, and Lily Larson. My writing partner, Judith Wise, also read and responded to draft after draft. Thanks, Judy.

Thanks to Red Adept Publishing, who has published two of my novels during this time. I love the community of authors and the quality of the books you publish. Because of your outstanding editorial and other support, I'm the proud parent of Who She Is and If She Had Stayed.

Thanks to my brother, David Byington, who lived through the experiences in "When It's Your Time" with me. And thanks always to my dear husband, Daniel Booth, whose support means everything to me.

ABOUT THE AUTHOR

Diane Byington

Diane Byington began writing fiction after she retired from her career as a social work college professor and psychotherapist. She does her best to combine her love of trying to understand people with her passion for writing their stories. In addition to writing short stories, Diane has published two novels: Who She Is and If She Had Stayed.

Besides writing, Diane loves to read, kayak, photograph sunsets, paint with acrylics, and weave. She used to raise Angora goats for fiber but sold them when she realized she'd need several lifetimes to spin and weave all the fiber she already had.

Diane and her husband divide their time between Boulder, Colorado, and Dunedin, Florida.

Check out Diane's website: www.dianebyington.com

and feel free to leave a message. Join her newsletter for information about Diane's future projects. Also, if you like these stories, leaving a short review on Amazon or another online retailer might earn you your angel's wings.

Follow Diane on Facebook (https://www.facebook.com/dianebyingtonauthor), Twitter (https://twitter.com/dianebyington), or Instagram (https://www.instagram.com/dianebbyington).

BOOKS BY THIS AUTHOR

Who She Is

In the fall of 1967, Faye Smith's family moves to Florida to work in the orange groves, and she has to start a new school... again. She tries out for the track team, knowing her mother would never approve because of Faye's epilepsy.

When Faye discovers she has a talent for distance running, she and her friend Francie decide to enter the Boston Marathon, even though women aren't allowed to compete. Desperate to climb out of the rut of poverty, Faye is determined to take part and win a college scholarship.

After the school bully tries to run her down with his car, a strange memory surfaces—a scene Faye doesn't recognize. Her parents insist that it's a symptom of her epilepsy, but Faye thinks they might be lying, especially when it keeps happening. To get her life on the right path, she'll need to figure out what her parents are hiding and never lose sight of the finish line.

If She Had Stayed

Sometimes the past is better left alone.

Kaley Kline is thrilled to have landed a job as director of the new Tesla Museum in Colorado Springs. To make the museum successful, she searches for undiscovered works to display. When she finds an old safe that might have been Tesla's, she's shocked to find some diary pages supposedly written by the inventor himself.

Kaley initially thinks either that the journal is a fraud or Tesla was experiencing a nervous breakdown when he wrote it. However, if his experiments were real, the world will never be the same. She decides to secretly build Tesla's time machine and attempt to go back into her own life to change a decision she has always regretted.

She prepares for a trip to the past, not knowing whether she will electrocute herself or travel back to the Boulder of her sophomore year in college. But an old boyfriend might have hidden some secrets from her—secrets that could have her fighting for her life.